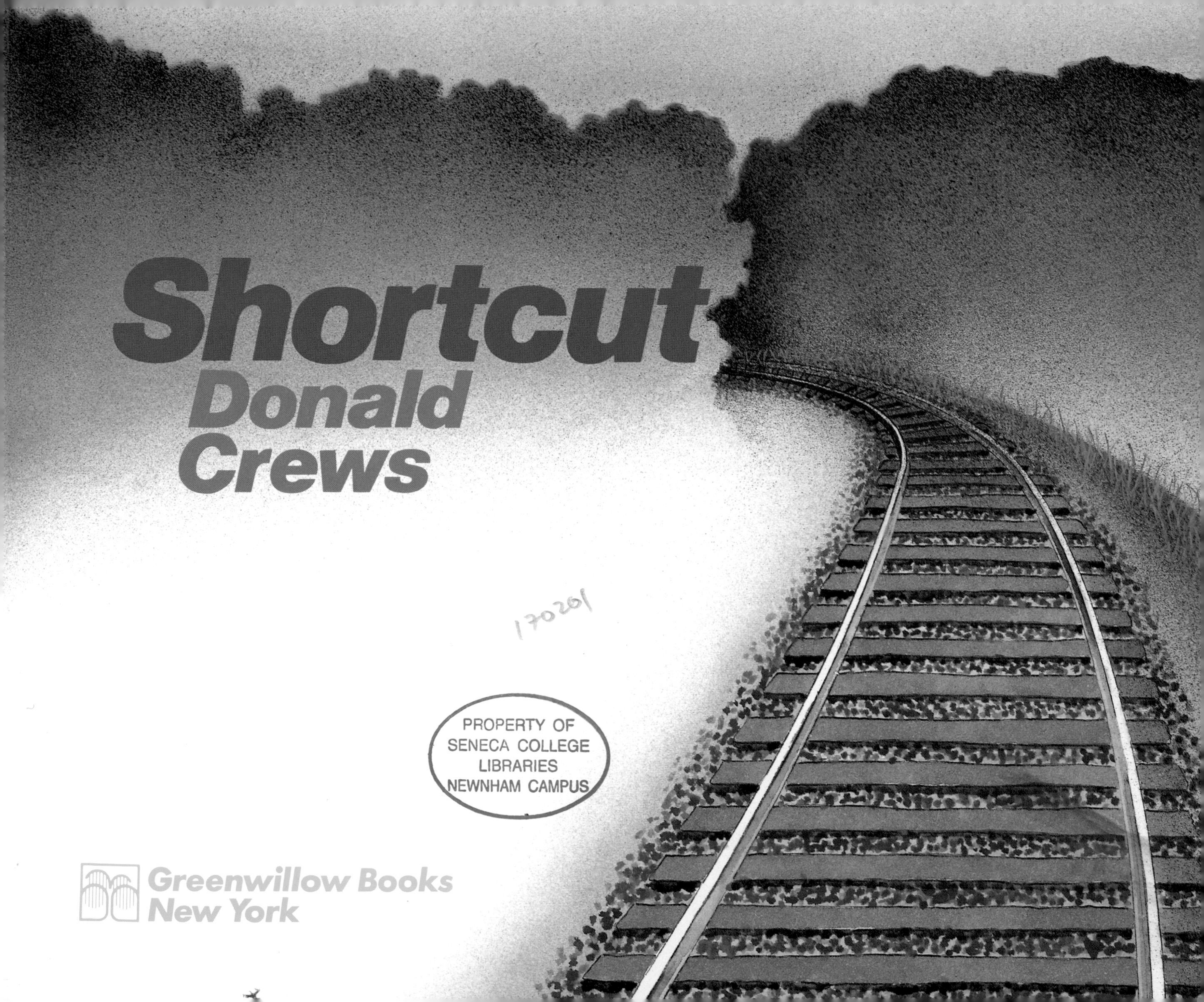

Shortcut

Donald Crews

Greenwillow Books
New York

Watercolor and gouache
paints were used for
the full-color art.
An airbrush was
used for accents.
The text type is
Futura Bold Italic.

Shortcut
Copyright © 1992
by Donald Crews
All rights reserved.
Manufactured in China.
www.harperchildrens.com
First Edition 15 14 13 12 11

Library of Congress
Cataloging-in-Publication Data
Crews, Donald.
Shortcut/by Donald Crews.
p. cm.
"Greenwillow Books."
Summary:
Children taking a shortcut
by walking along a
railroad track find
excitement and danger
when a train approaches.

ISBN 0-688-06436-1
ISBN 0-688-06437-X (lib.)
ISBN 0-688-13576-5 (pbk.)
[1. Railroads—Fiction.
2. Afro-Americans—Fiction.]
I. Title.
PZ7.C8682Sh 1992
[E]—dc20
91-36312   CIP   AC

To Mama/Daddy

Brother/Shirley
Mary
Sylvester/Edward
Sylvia

All's well
that
ends well

We looked....
We listened....
We decided to take
the shortcut home.

We should have taken the road.
But it was late, and it was
getting dark, so we
started down the track.

We knew when the passenger trains
passed. But the freight trains
didn't run on schedule.
They might come at any time.

We should have taken the road.

**The track ran along a mound.
Its steep slopes were covered
with briers. There was
water at the bottom, surely
full of snakes.**

**We laughed. We shouted. We sang.
We tussled. We threw stones.
We passed the cut-off that
led back to the road.**

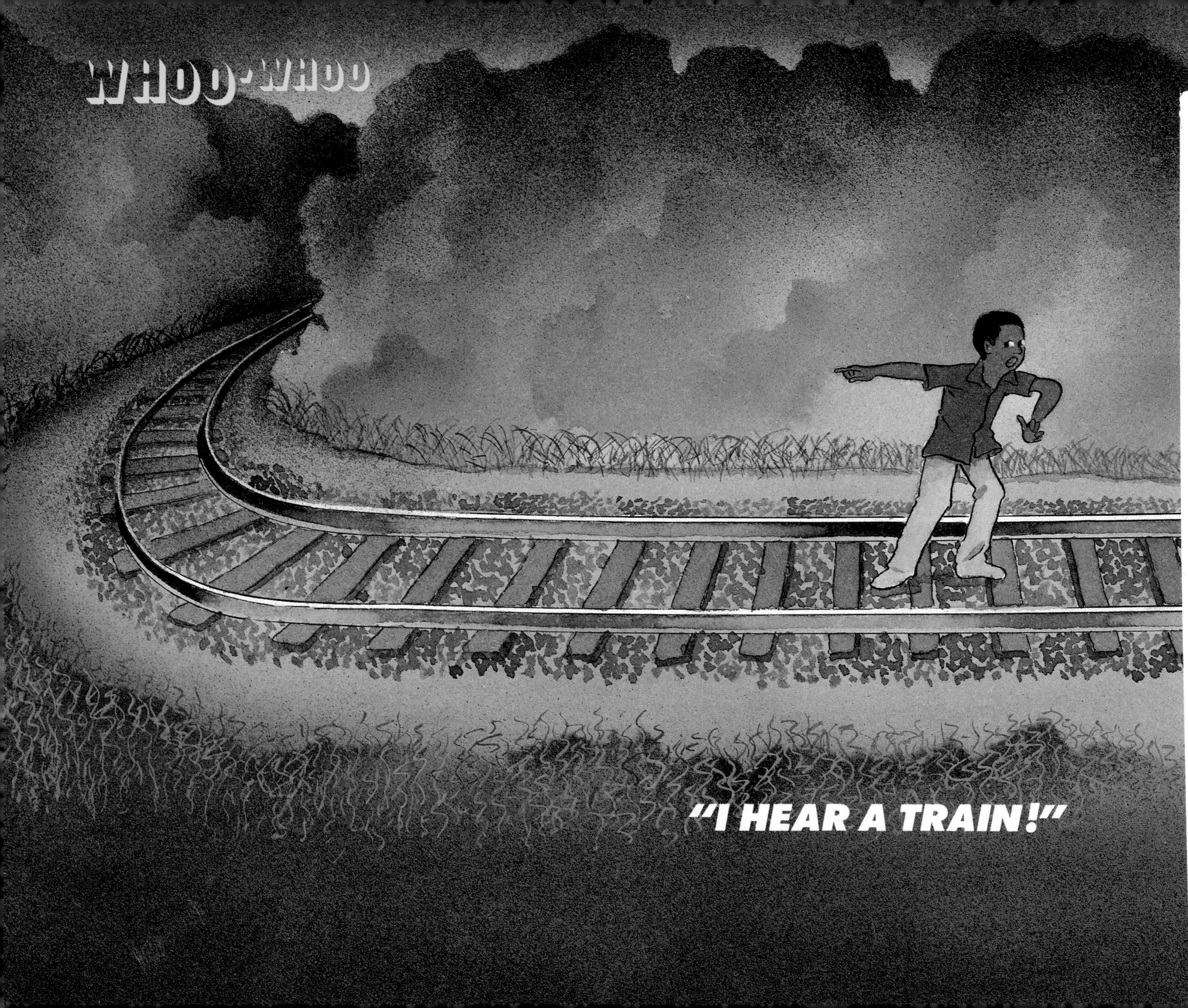

WHOO-WHOO

"I HEAR A TRAIN!"

Everybody stopped.
Everybody listened.

We all heard the train whistle.
Should we run ahead to the
path home or back to the cut-off?

The train whistle was *much louder.*

"Back to the cut-off!"   "RUN"

We jumped off the tracks onto the steep slope. We didn't think about the briers or the snakes.

KLAKITY-KLAKITY

KLAKITY-KLAK

The train passed.
We were all fine.
We climbed back onto the tracks.
We hurried to the cut-off
and onto the road.

We walked home without a word.
We didn't tell Bigmama. We didn't tell Mama.
We didn't tell anyone. We didn't talk about
what had happened for a very long time.
And we didn't take the shortcut again.